DILYS P

NORMAN
PRICE

BELLA
LASAGNE

JAMES

SARAH

MEET ALL THESE FRIENDS IN BUZZ BOOKS:

Thomas the Tank Engine
Tiny Toon Adventures
Looney Tunes
Bugs Bunny
Fireman Sam
Joshua Jones
Toucan 'Tecs
Flintstones
Jetsons

First published 1991 by Buzz Books,
an imprint of Reed International Books Ltd
Michelin House, 81 Fulham Road, London SW3 6RB
Reprinted 1992

LONDON MELBOURNE AUCKLAND

Fireman Sam © 1985 Prism Art & Design Ltd

Text © 1991 William Heinemann Ltd
Illustrations © 1991 William Heinemann Ltd
Based on the animation series produced by Bumper Films
for S4C/Channel 4 Wales and Prism Art & Design Ltd.
Original idea by Dave Gingell and Dave Jones,
assisted by Mike Young. Characters created by Rob Lee.
All rights reserved.

ISBN 1 85591 108 6

Printed and bound in the UK by BPCC Hazell Books Ltd

LOST IN THE FOG

Story by Caroline Hill-Trevor
Developed from a storyline by Rob Lee
and a script by Nia Ceidiog
Illustrations by The County Studio

"It's not fair, this isn't," moaned Norman, as he mopped the shop floor. "It was an accident . . . honest."

"Accident my foot!" Dilys scoffed. "I suppose those stink bombs just appeared out of thin air!"

"But Mam, I'm going to Penny Morris's for tea with Sarah and James . . ."

"No, Norman, you're not getting away with it this time."

Meanwhile, Fireman Sam and Elvis were driving back to Pontypandy after a call out.

"Cloud's coming down thick over the valley," said Fireman Sam, turning on Jupiter's headlights.

Later, Dilys was reading her horoscope at
Bella's cafe.

"A load of rubbish zey are," said Bella.

"No they're not – I always read mine,"
said Dilys. "I read the tea leaves too," she
added peering into Bella's empty cup. "Mrs
Lasagne," she said, "you will meet a dark
handsome man who loves to travel."

Sarah who had overheard Dilys, was impressed. "Tell my fortune, please, Mrs Price," she begged.

"I can't read tea leaves from milk shakes," said Dilys, "but . . . swill this cup out." She handed Sarah the cup she'd just finished with. "Ah . . . um, I see you going on a journey this afternoon," said Dilys.

"Wow! Go on, Mrs Price," urged James.

"To Newtown . . . oh dear, it's misting over now . . ."

"I think crystal balls do that, no, Mrs Price?" asked Bella suspiciously, but as Trevor came into the cafe she joked, "Perhaps Mr Evans is my handsome travelling man!"

"What did I tell you?" said Dilys. "I've got the gift!   And it looks as though you'll come to a sticky end, Sarah," Dilys continued, watching Sarah wipe the jam off her face with her hanky.

"Come on you two," said Trevor. "Time for us to go."

11

"Bye, Uncle Sam," called Sarah and James, waving as Jupiter passed Trevor's bus.

"Can we get out here, please?" asked Sarah, when they got up into the hills. "We want to pick some daisies for Penny."

Trevor looked at the cloud and frowned.

"Don't worry," said Sarah. "We can walk from here. It's not far to Newtown."

"All right then, but be careful," he called out. The twins had already climbed over the gate into a field.

"Hurry up Sarah, or we'll be late for tea," shouted James impatiently.

"Just a few more," called Sarah.

By now, the cloud had turned into fog. It was getting thicker and thicker.

Back at the shop, Norman was still cleaning.

"I'm no good at this," he moaned as a sack of budgie seed toppled over.

"You need the practice then," said Dilys crossly. "If only I could have seen what the future held for me," she muttered.

"I bet Penny will take Sarah and James to the pictures after tea," said Norman with a sigh, as he picked up the broom again. "And here's me slavin' away at home!"

Dilys grinned to herself as she overheard what Norman was saying.

"There we are," said Sarah, holding up a big bunch of daisies. "Let's go."

"Yes, or we'll miss the film," James agreed. "Oh . . . I can't see the gate."

"Don't be such a baby, it's over there!"

"No, it's not," James replied nervously.

Sarah looked around. "Oh dear, you're right for once. Now what can we do?"

The twins wandered around, searching for the way back to the road.

"Aagh! What's that?" screamed Sarah.

"Only a tree, silly," whispered James. "Everything looks different in the fog – isn't it spooky?"

"Strange," said Penny, peering out of the window into the fog. "Sarah and James should be here by now. I'd better call Pontypandy and see what's happened."

"Well, I don't know, but I did see them in the bus with Trevor," said Fireman Sam when Penny rang.

"Newtown's hidden by fog," said Penny. "They must be lost."

"We'd better go and look for them," said Fireman Sam. "I'll meet you halfway along the Newtown road, Penny."

"Rightio, Sam. Drive carefully," said Penny and she set out in Venus.

"Fireman Sam to Firefighter Penny Morris. Over," said Fireman Sam as he drove slowly with Jupiter's headlights on.

"I can't see much, Sam. Oh! Here are some headlights."

"Hang on, Penny, here's a car!"

Fireman Sam slammed on the brakes.

"Oh! It's Jupiter," exclaimed Penny.

The two vehicles stopped just in time.

"Phew, that was lucky!" said Penny, jumping out of Venus.

"Very," agreed Fireman Sam. "Now, where have Sarah and James got to?"

"Look," said Penny pointing to the gate.

"Sarah's hanky," said Fireman Sam. "They went through the gate."

21

"Right," said Fireman Sam, "you stay with the vehicles while I go and look." He picked up his torch and set off.

"Sar-ah! Ja-ames! Where are you?"

Fireman Sam's voice echoed as he made his way down the track in the fog.

22

"It's all your fault we're lost," James complained.

"No it's not!" Sarah argued as she stumbled forward. "Oh, help James!"

"You've fallen into the marsh! Quick, grab my hand," cried James.

"I'm going under!" cried Sarah.

"Don't panic Sarah. H-E-L-P!"

Fireman Sam stopped in his tracks.

"Sarah! James! I'm on my way," he called back. He started running in the direction of their cries.

"Great Fires of London! I can't go forward, or I'll sink too," said Fireman Sam.

"Any luck, Fireman Sam?" said Penny over the radio.

"We need your help. Drive down the track," Fireman Sam replied.

"Message received and understood. I'm on my way," said Penny calmly.

Penny drove Venus towards Sarah and
fixed one end of a rope round the winch.
She gave the other end to Fireman Sam.

"Right Sarah," said Fireman Sam,
throwing the rope out to Sarah. "Catch the
rope and put the loop under your arms."

They all waited nervously.

"Got it!" yelled Sarah, after a few tries.

"Well done," said Fireman Sam with
relief. "Start winching, Penny."

Very slowly, the rope was pulled tight
and eventually Sarah was pulled out of the
boggy ground, into Fireman Sam's arms.

"Thanks, Penny," said James, and he
handed Penny the bunch of daisies that
Sarah had dropped.

27

Back at the cafe, Sarah and James were tucking into Bella's special pizza when Dilys walked in, followed by Norman.

"What are you two doing here? You're supposed to be at the pictures," exclaimed Dilys, surprised.

"How did you know that?" asked Sarah.

"Oh . . . I just know," Dilys sighed.

"I told you this morning, you mean," said Norman. "Remember, Mam?"

Dilys turned round and glared at Norman.

"Oh dear! Norman's future is looking dim!" giggled Sarah and they all laughed at the joke.

FIREMAN SAM

STATION OFFICER STEELE

TREVOR EVANS

ELVIS CRIDLINGTON

PENNY MORRIS